Claws

Stephen Booth

CRIME EXPRESS

Claws

by *Stephen Booth*

Published by Crime Express in 2007
Crime Express is an imprint of
Five Leaves Publications,
PO Box 8787, Nottingham NG1 9AW

ISBN: 978-1-905512-24-9

Crime Express 2

Five Leaves acknowledges financial support
from Arts Council England

Five Leaves is a member of Inpress
(www.inpressbooks.co.uk),
representing independent publishers

Typesetting and design:
Four Sheets Design and Print

Printed in Great Britain

1.

The bones were tiny. They lay in his hand like a set of pearls, translucent and fragile. When he turned them to the light, he could see their fractured ends and hollow cores. They were light as a feather, as brittle as chalk. And as easy to break as a straw.

For a moment, Detective Constable Ben Cooper stared at the narrow window and faded curtains, though they hid nothing more than a street corner in a Derbyshire mining town. He was trying to picture a shape coming out of nowhere, a shadow against the sun. He could almost feel the sudden grab, hear the sharp snap. A broken back, he guessed. Dead in an instant.

Cooper looked up. Had he spoken that last thought out loud? PC Tracy Udall had been watching him handle the bones, her expression suggesting he might do something against procedure at any moment. His secondment to the Rural Crime Squad had given him a kind of loose cannon status in Udall's eyes. He was the rogue element that no one quite controlled.

"Where did you say these were found, Tracy?" he asked.

Udall nodded at the opposite wall. "In a Tupperware box. They were stuffed in a drawer, with his underwear and socks."

She said it as if the socks made the presence of bones worse, somehow. A casual attitude to death was always disturbing. No one could tolerate a life tossed away like so much rubbish.

As usual, Udall was in full uniform, her duty belt loaded with equipment that rucked her yellow high-vis jacket into untidy folds over her waist. Handcuffs, baton, CS spray. And a series of leather pouches that Cooper had forgotten the use for. In fact, he didn't think there had been all those items to carry when he was in uniform.

Changes happened fast in Derbyshire Constabulary, and six years in CID werea long enough to get out of touch with core policing.

"But at least they're only a handful of bones," said Udall. "Less than a handful."

The only thing she'd taken off was her hat, which she laid carefully on a chair, a gesture to informality. In the enclosed space, she had to stand very close. And despite the six-inch difference in their heights, Cooper found her slightly intimidating.

This had been an unremarkable bedroom once — one of those tiny spaces that was no more than a box room. There was just enough distance between the walls to fit a bed, and a chest of drawers under the window. He'd slept in a bedroom like this himself as a child, back at Bridge End Farm. But some youngsters spent their entire lives in a space this size.

"I suppose he didn't have much interest in bones," he said.

"No. They weren't one of his *special* trophies."

Downstairs, officers from Serious Crime could be heard moving through the rooms, checking the kitchen, breaking open the shed in the back yard. They'd raided the house in response to intelligence that it was being used to stash the proceeds of activities by local drug dealers who were being targeted in a major police operation. It was the sort of place they might find to keep their money safe until the attention died down. The officer in charge downstairs had hopes of finding a couple of hundred grand hidden under the floorboards, or stuffed into coffee tins, the way a southern force had in a similar raid a while ago.

Cooper turned slowly and studied the room. It couldn't be called a bedroom any more. There was no bed in it, for a start — only a series of glass-fronted cabinets, a small table, and a single chair. Some of the contents of the cabinets were difficult to make out, unfamiliar shapes under a gathering layer of dust. Shoeboxes and biscuit tins had been crammed into the rest of the available space, and two suitcases lay open on the floor.

Cooper put the bones down, feeling oddly disturbed by the way they slid and rustled in their evidence bag, like the last few crumbs in a packet of biscuits.

"Prey, I suppose," he said.

Udall nodded. "Aren't they all?"

She was strangely quiet this morning. Cooper wondered if some issue in her personal life had come too close to the surface. Tracy Udall had two small children at home, and he gathered that the father had been absent from the word go. Present for the conception, maybe, but missing for the birth. Udall was as professional as they came, but even police officers were human.

"A small species of some kind," he said. "It would have been taken by the male, then dismembered later on. You wouldn't think there'd be much flesh on it, would you? Enough to keep a few hungry mouths quiet for a while. But that's all."

"Every scrap is important when you're a parent."

"I see. Well… maybe I don't."

"One day, Ben."

Between them, the boxes and suitcases in this room contained a collection of several thousand eggs. Nestling between layers of cotton wool were the speckled pale greens and blues of bullfinches, redstarts and wheatears, the creamy white of a woodpecker. There were the blotched, chestnut red of the peregrine, and goshawk eggs the colour of the moon. Each item had been recorded in a notebook, with the date, time and location of the acquisition. Every egg had been labelled in precise black letters, and its insides had been blown out through a tiny hole drilled in its side. There had been a lifetime of work in these dead things.

Cooper could see other items, too — fleshless skulls, clawed feet, severed wings. Some people liked to collect the skeletons of dead birds. But avian bones were so light and fragile they soon fell apart, and all you found was a skull. A collector hoped for a fledgling to die in the nest. Only then could you retrieve a complete skeleton, if you were lucky.

"I reckon our egg thief just scooped the entire contents out of a nest," said Udall.

"He seems to have picked up practically anything he could find."

"Yes. You might call him a bit of a magpie."

Relieved, Cooper felt the tension ease, without knowing what had caused it in the first place.

"He's a genuine collector, certainly. Obsessive, I'd say. Real collectors always seem slightly unbalanced to the rest of us."

"As if the rest of us are normal, Ben?" Udall sighed. "Yes, you're right. And that'll probably count in his favour with the courts, if we ever get him that far."

"What do you mean?"

"Well, we can't prove he was engaged in this activity for personal gain."

"He wasn't dealing?"

"Not so far as we can tell. By the look of this room, he seems to have held on to everything he found, no matter how worthless and bizarre."

Cooper picked up the file Udall had given him, and frowned at the mug shot on the first page. Kevin Hewitt, aged forty-two, an unemployed van driver.

"Single, I'd guess," he said. "Oh... no, I'm wrong. Separated from his wife."

"That's worse than single," said Udall, with feeling.

Leaning past her, Cooper examined the aluminium cage that stood on the table. The whole room could have done with fumigating, but the area around the cage smelled worst of all.

"And this was Mr Hewitt's most special trophy, I suppose," he said.

"You could call it that. It makes me sick to look at it."

The goshawk chick had been very young. How anyone had imagined they could keep it alive in an old parrot cage in a box room was beyond belief. Now it lay in a pathetic heap, its eyes glazed with death, its beak gaping to show a glimpse of red tongue. The debris around it on the soiled newspaper would be difficult to identify. It might be interesting to know what Hewitt had been trying to feed the chick with, but it made no difference in the long run.

Cooper looked at Udall. "Definitely a goshawk? I can't tell at this age."

"Sergeant Jackson will be here soon to confirm it. Then we'll get the remains to the lab to do a cross-check against the DNA database."

"But ten to one it's a wild bird, snatched from the nest?"

"Oh, a hundred to one," said Udall. "A

thousand to one."

The young raptor could be called beautiful, even in death. There was a kind of elegance in the angle of the head, and the way the feathers lay. Its legs were stretched out, as if reaching for its prey. Yet it would never have seen prey, except at second hand, delivered half-digested from its mother's beak. Those talons had been made to ride currents of air over Alport Castles crags in the Upper Derwent Valley, not to lie on a filthy sheet of paper in a collector's trophy room.

Cooper studied the young goshawk closely before he straightened up to his full height and faced Udall again.

"And where is Mr Hewitt now?"

"Well, that," said Udall, "is what we have to find out."

Kevin Hewitt was already too high, and he was sweating badly. A hot trickle ran down his forehead, and another dripped into his shirt. He didn't have a hand free to wipe it away, so the perspiration was already in his eyes, blurring his vision and making him blink. He stopped for a rest, digging the gaffs of his irons into the bark and clutching a branch for support. He was breathing hard, and he could feel pains starting to shoot through his shoulders.

"Damn, she was right. I *am* getting too old for this."

The only response was an angry, high-pitched cry from the bird circling above the tree. A coarse *gyak, gyak, gyak*, telling the world there was a disturbance near her nest. The bird was way up in the sky, almost too far for Hewitt to see, even if he could use the binoculars. But he knew she was watching him, her eyes so much sharper than his, observing his slightest movement.

At this time of year, the female wouldn't hesitate to attack him, if he got too close. Three pounds of angry female goshawk were quite a scary thought. The beak was fearsome enough, but you didn't want to tangle with those talons. They were designed for tearing lumps of meat off warm prey.

The male bird, the tercel, would be away hunting, soaring invisibly over the conifer plantations, or flicking among the trees, twisting and turning

12

in pursuit of some prey on the ground. When Hewitt imagined the strike, the talons sinking into fur, he knew why people wanted these birds. Goshawks had short, powerful wings that made them manoeuvrable in dense woodland. But they were totally focused on their prey, and sometimes they collided with obstacles. He'd heard of one collector who stumbled across a stunned bird in the woods and snatched it up before it flew off again. Lucky bugger. It would never happen to him. Kevin Hewitt had to work for everything he got.

Hewitt's common sense was telling him he'd climbed too far. But he couldn't go back, not now. He coughed as a scatter of dirt fell on his face and into his mouth. That was the story of his life. Going out on a limb for people who always let him down, who'd leave him to crash and burn. When his end came, everyone would stand and watch him fall. No one would care what happened to him. Whether he ended up spending a few months in the nick, or lying down there on those rocks, with his neck broken. What was the difference?

Cautiously, Hewitt inched further along the branch, wincing as a patch of bark bit through his jeans. Even that movement shifted his balance, and he had to clutch at the rope fastened to the trunk. For a few seconds, he wobbled dangerously. His hands shook, and his palms were slippery with sweat. What he really needed was a safety harness, the kind that tree surgeons used. But there was no way he could carry a thing like that around, not without some nosey sod asking what he was up to. The climbing irons were tricky enough to hide.

Of course, if he was caught, there'd definitely be a prison sentence this time. They might even impound his old Bedford van, and then he'd really be sunk.

But it was worse than that. If he landed in jail, Janine would do what she'd threatened and file for divorce next day. She'd get to keep the kids, too. No doubt about that. Women had it all their own way in family courts. They could refuse access and ignore as many court orders as they liked — and they were never punished for it. If he blew his last chance with Janine, he'd never see Jack and Ebony again. He might as well throw himself in the reservoir if that happened.

Hewitt glanced over his shoulder. Yes, Howden was nice and handy down there. Plenty deep enough at the moment, too. He could just imagine himself taking a header off that stupid bloody dam, the one they'd built to look like a castle, with its towers and battlements.

For a moment, he thought of the male goshawk, returning to a favourite perch after a successful attack on some unsuspecting rabbit, then plucking it and pulling out the entrails before it ate the meat. That was the way he could see himself ending up. Not like the hawk, flying free over the moor. But like the poor bloody rabbit, gutted and skinned.

Hewitt sighed. "Onward and upward, damn it."

He began to move again, slowly and painfully, peering up into the leaves. The nest was up there somewhere, he was sure. It was almost within his grasp, if only he could see it.

"A goshawk chick all right. They can tear up their own food at about a month old, but this one is only just starting to feather."

Sergeant Phil Jackson was approaching thirty

years' service, and no doubt counting the days to his full pension. He looked as though he'd been round the block a few times in his thirty. More than a few. Cooper had taken a liking to him immediately.

"It's a pity, but it's practically impossible to keep the breeding sites of rare species a secret," said Jackson, as he removed the dead goshawk from its cage. "Word gets around, and twitchers turn up in their hundreds. The only thing that works is guarding nests day and night, and no one has the resources to do that."

Cooper was standing at the window, looking down into the street. This was an ordinary terraced house — a typical council property, identical to thousands of others on the eastern borders of Derbyshire. A cluster of spectators had gathered in the street, drawn from their houses by the sight of police activity. Actual miners might still live in some of these homes, men who were working the handful of pits left over from the closures of the 80s and 90s.

He could see that the Serious Crime team were starting to leave already. There had been no stash of money in Kevin Hewitt's house, then. No wedges of used notes under the floorboards, nothing stuffed in the coffee tins except coffee. Not even a sniff from the Springer spaniel that was now being loaded back into his van. The team would be off to raid another property somewhere, probably. Some officers enjoyed the smash and grab jobs, preferred to leave the legwork to someone else. Cooper didn't mind that.

"And birds of prey are particularly at risk, Sergeant?" he asked.

"Oh, yes — and the rarer the better, as far as collectors are concerned. At one time, the fashion was to stuff raptors and mount them on a perch in your sitting room. Then eggs became the target. As long as there's money to be made, birds of prey will be killed."

"Supply and demand."

"Like anything else."

Jackson was a wildlife liaison officer working with the Peak Nestwatch project. He was also South Yorkshire Police, but county boundaries were meaningless up on the moors of the Dark Peak.

Thanks to Tracy Udall, Cooper knew the basics of Nestwatch. The Upper Derwent Valley was an area that had been associated with birds of prey for a long time. Until the 1960s, they'd been absent for more than a century, eliminated by pesticides and persecution. Then the goshawk had returned to breed, followed by peregrine falcons. For twenty or thirty years, visitors had been able to watch them displaying in the spring over the Alport Castle crags. The fastest birds in Britain, graceful and spectacular.

But alarm bells had rung in 2001, when just one goshawk chick survived from eleven nests, and adult birds vanished from the valley. It had been impossible to tell what was happening, because most of the land was in private ownership. But something had to be done. The result was Pak Nestwatch, a partnership between the police and bodies like the RSPB and the national park.

"So is the situation improving?" asked Cooper.

"Changing, anyway," said Jackson. "When the powers of imprisonment came in, serial egg collectors took a step back. It wasn't a question of a twenty-quid fine any more. Collectors knew they could go down."

"So — ?"

"So they took one of two routes. They either gave up altogether, or they decided it would have to be worth the risk they were taking."

"The stakes were raised."

"Exactly." Jackson looked up, assessing him with a cool blue eye. "Are you interested? We can always do with some help."

"Anything I can do, Sergeant."

"If you've got time later, I'll show you the hide we use."

"I go off duty at five."

"Fine."

Jackson turned his attention back to the goshawk. The bird's down was thick and woolly, but when Jackson ran his thumb across it, Cooper could see the first adult plumage — dark, transverse bands on the flight feathers, longitudinal markings on the wing coverts. Within a few more days, those feathers would have been strong enough to take the bird into the air, and even Kevin Hewitt wouldn't have caught it.

The legs had only a tinge of the bright yellow characteristic of the adult. Later, the eyes would have turned that piercing orange-yellow that gave the goshawk such an evil appearance. If it was a male bird, it would have developed the dark band behind the eyes that made it look even more fearsome. But the strength of the feet and talons was already obvious, and the sharp hook of the beak was unmistakeable.

"There's only a window of about two and a half weeks between feeding themselves, and their first flight," said Jackson. "Mr Hewitt took one too young. A pity the cameras didn't pick him up at the time."

"Oh, yes, the cameras."

Nestwatch had introduced high-tech surveillance techniques at an early stage. One year, live CCTV pictures had been transmitted direct from a goshawk nest to the Fairholmes visitor centre.

In the street, two youths looked up and saw him. Cooper let the curtain fall back. Just as in every town centre, offenders intent on raiding protected nest sites had learned to wear a hood or a hat in front of cameras to prevent identification.

Nestwatch had responded by taking samples of DNA from the feathers of birds of prey and setting up a database to identify stolen specimens.

Sergeant Jackson had turned the dead bird over, lifting one of the bare yellow legs.

"See the ring?" he said.

"Yes, I noticed that."

"A Schedule 4 bird bred in captivity has to be fitted with a ring issued by DEFRA, and stamped with a serial number. The ring is what distinguishes it from a wild bird. You have to put it on the chick soon after hatching. It passes over the foot, and becomes impossible to remove intact once the bird grows."

"But this bird has a ring. Doesn't that mean it's captive bred?"

"No. In goshawks, there's a difference in size between the male and female birds, so there are two sizes of ring. The normal practice is to fit both rings until a chick's sex becomes apparent — and that isn't until it's fledged. Then the wrong ring is removed. This particular bird is too young for anyone to be able to judge its sex. Yet it only has one ring."

"Can we check the serial number?"

"I've already done it. This ring was issued by DEFRA four years ago. The captive bird it was made for would be fully adult by now." Jackson shook his head. "You know, if this wild bird had reached adulthood, Mr Hewitt might have got away with it. Abuses can only be detected if there's a visible discrepancy between the ringed bird and its registered age. But when it's an obvious juvenile — ."

"I see. So if he got a ring on it, he must have taken the bird from the nest just after it hatched."

"Yes."

"Which means he managed to keep it alive for a while."

"Three or four weeks, I'd say."

The newly hatched goshawk would have been a sitting target for Kevin Hewitt. Cooper could picture him smiling as he peered over the edge of the nest, reaching in a hand to pick out a chick with silky white down and half-closed eyes, scarcely able to lift its head.

"So he used a fraudulent ring? But, Sergeant, you said just now these rings can't be removed."

"Well, that wasn't quite true," admitted Jackson. "There is *one* way that a ring can be removed intact."

"What way is that?"

"By cutting off the bird's leg."

"Damn."

Jackson stared at him grimly. "Yes. Let's hope the captive hawk had already died a natural death."

Janine Hewitt was just leaving her front door when Cooper and Udall arrived on the Devonshire housing estate. She had one child in a pushchair, and a boy of about four trailing behind. According to her husband's record, there was an older son, presumably at school. Janine looked a good few years younger than Kevin — not much more than thirty, but thin and gaunt-eyed, like a woman old before her time.

"Going somewhere, Mrs Hewitt?" asked Udall, subtly placing herself in the woman's path, forcing her to slow down.

"We're off to the park for an hour. Nothing wrong with that, is there?" she said.

"Giving the kids a bit of fresh air? Well, it's not a bad day for it."

"It's for me," said Janine. "It drives me crazy being cooped up in the house all day. You've no idea what it's like. One of these mornings, I'm going to lose it completely and go mental. Then you lot would have reason to come round quick, I reckon."

"We'll walk with you," said Cooper.

"Please yourselves."

The older child stared at the police officers as they walked across the road. He clung to his mother's hand, but showed little interest in her. Udall's uniform seemed to fascinate him instead.

"We're looking for Kevin, you know," said Udall. "We need to locate him urgently."

Janine didn't answer. They entered a small recreation area — a stretch of grass grown slightly too long since the council last cut it, two lines of wooden benches facing each other, a few shrubs and flower beds, a fenced playground where children clambered on a slide.

"Did you hear me, Mrs Hewitt?"

"Yes, you're looking for Kevin. Isn't everybody?"

Cooper and Udall exchanged glances. "Has someone else been asking about him?"

Janine settled herself on a bench. Not the first bench or the second, but the third seat along the path, with a view of the playground, near an old iron drinking fountain. She chose it as if it was routine, regardless of the fact that all the other benches were empty.

"There were some other coppers here this morning. They searched my house," she said.

"That would be Serious Crime."

"They said they were looking for money. Money? Do I look as though I have a secret wad of dosh? What's it all about?"

"Well, what did they tell you?"

"They didn't tell me anything. It looks like you're not going to, either. It doesn't make any sense."

"Mrs Hewitt, where is your husband?" asked Udall.

"I don't know," said Janine, sounding almost relieved that she was finally able to make sense of what she was being asked.

"When did you last see him?"

"He hasn't been around for weeks. Three weeks, at least. I don't know exactly. I'm not his keeper. We don't live together any more."

"Yes, we know that. But he keeps in touch, surely? He visits the children from time to time?"

"Sometimes. But, like I said — ."

" — you haven't seen him for three weeks. Is that what you said?"

Cooper watched Janine Hewitt closely while Udall questioned her. After a few minutes, she began to get nervous.

"I don't have to answer any more questions," she said. "It's upsetting the kids."

"You'll let us know if you hear from Kevin," said Cooper, handing her his card.

At first he didn't think she was going to take it, but politeness seemed to get the better of her, and she shoved the card into her pocket.

"I'm off," she said.

"It was a short visit to the park, Janine."

"I didn't like the atmosphere."

The four-year-old seemed disappointed when

his mother dragged him away. Cooper felt warm, and looked at the drinking fountain. But he could see there had been no water in it for decades.

"Who else do we have on the list, Tracy?" he asked.

"A fellow egg collector, Gareth Stark. We think he was Hewitt's partner at one time."

"So what happened? Did they fall out?"

"Stark got caught in possession and did three months. He claims to have given up egg collecting now."

"And become a law-abiding citizen?"

"We'll see."

They walked back to the car, which they'd been careful to leave in sight — a vital precaution on the Devonshire Estate.

"Did you believe Janine Hewitt when she said she hadn't seen Kevin for three weeks?" asked Udall.

"She didn't quite say that. Didn't you notice? She answered you obliquely — she said Kevin 'hadn't been around'. Evading a direct answer is a classic sign of a lie."

Udall nodded. "I should have pressed her on it."

"It wouldn't have done any good. You'd just have forced her to lie directly. Then she would have resented us, and we'd lose her co-operation altogether."

"Co-operation? Is that what you'd call it?"

"She did speak to us," said Cooper. "Around here, that means we're practically best friends."

2.

Gareth Stark had been brought into the police station at Edendale. He was sitting in Interview Room Two with a plastic cup in a paper napkin, staring at the coffee in disgust. He had long, thin fingers and a mane of dark hair that was probably tied into a pony tail when he wanted to look trendy.

His expression changed from disgust to outrage when he heard Udall's first question.

"I wasn't just some egg collector, my dear," he said. "I was an oologist. For me, it was a question of scientific study."

"Oh, of course."

Cooper suspected that calling Tracy Udall 'my

dear' was likely to earn Stark a crack on the head with her side-handled baton if he wasn't careful. But Stark seemed oblivious. He looked from one to the other, and a curl came to his lip.

"Without the early collectors, we wouldn't possess half the knowledge about bird species that we do now. And there wouldn't be specimens in the museums for future generations to study."

"But those collectors did all the work," suggested Cooper. "We don't need any more specimens now."

"How do you know?" said Stark quickly.

"Fair enough, sir. We don't."

The lack of argument seemed to deflate him.

"What about your partner, Kevin Hewitt?" asked Udall.

"Partner?" Stark laughed. "Kevin was useful, that's all. He could climb trees. And he developed a sort of sly talent for avoiding getting caught. An instinctive cunning. But he never had the brains. Kevin *was* just a collector. Too obsessive, too greedy. Eventually, he was bound to make a mistake."

"But you were the one who got caught. You

received a three-month prison sentence."

Stark's face froze. "Not through my own mistake."

"And yet you didn't provide information against your partner. That was very loyal."

"Kevin wasn't — ." Stark stopped, and grimaced. "I know what you're doing. You're trying to provoke me. Well, it won't work. I'm here voluntarily, to provide information. I can leave any time I want to."

"Kevin is back to his old trade," said Cooper. "Did you know?"

"He would never have seen it as a trade. Egg collecting was always a passion for Kevin. He's never been driven by money."

"Well, Mr Hewitt seems to have lost his principles. He's working for money now. And we'd like to know who he's working for."

Stark gazed at the wall, and at first Cooper thought he wasn't going to respond. But then he sighed and slumped in his chair.

"He must be going after the peregrines, I suppose. Or is it goshawks?"

"How did you know that?" asked Udall.

"One of the first principles of egg collecting is 'the rarer the better'."

"Who would Kevin be working with now, Mr Stark? We need names."

"I have no idea. I lost touch with that world when I got the conviction. Suddenly, I became *persona non grata*. And don't ask me where Kevin will go. The birds he'll be looking for don't always use the same nests every year. Kevin will have found new sites. That's his skill. It's what he does."

"Not for much longer," said Cooper.

Back at his desk, Cooper opened Kevin Hewitt's file. Hewitt had a record of minor offences, mostly between the ages of fifteen and twenty-five. There had been spells of community service, probation and fines. Despite being a serial offender, he'd avoided prison. That was mostly because Hewitt had never been convicted of a violent offence. The prisons were too full to send away anyone except the most dangerous offenders.

Cooper put some actions in progress — an alert for the whereabouts of Hewitt's Bedford van, a request for his phone records, to see who he'd been calling in the past few days. Bank records would show if Hewitt was spending money or drawing cash out somewhere, but he'd need authorisation for those.

Jackson and Udall had provided intelligence on egg collectors and known associates of Hewitt's. Cooper felt sure he'd have more sense than to go to an address already known to the police, though. It wouldn't even take that instinctive cunning Gareth Stark had referred to.

A few minutes later, he saw Udall emerge from a meeting she'd been attending.

"Serious Crime still have Kevin Hewitt as a suspect, but he's dropped very low on their list," she said. "They think since the principle suspects came under scrutiny, they've been using people like Hewitt for their own purposes."

"Like stashing the proceeds?"

Udall nodded. "On the surface, he might not seem like the obvious choice."

"But that's a very good reason for choosing him, right?"

"Exactly. He could have been set up as a fall

guy, an expendable asset."

"Someone is doing a bit of strategic thinking at the top, then. It doesn't sound like a bunch of unemployed steel workers making a bit of pocket money, Tracy."

"No. I think that's why they're happy to leave Hewitt to us."

"So we're not off the enquiry?"

"Far from it. Do you know, they even asked if the Rural Crime Squad could mount a surveillance operation in the Upper Derwent."

"What, using CROPS?" asked Cooper.

"We have people trained in CROPS, of course. But have you seen the moors up there?"

"Yes. A bit exposed for covert rural observation points."

"You'd need to be able to disguise yourself as a grouse to pass unnoticed."

"From next month, a grouse would be the most dangerous thing you could look like, Tracy. They have a pretty short life span once the shooting season starts."

Udall sighed. "Country sports. I can't see the appeal. Give me dinner and a few glasses of wine in a nice restaurant any time."

Cooper looked down at his desk, wondering if he'd just been given a signal. Was he supposed to respond to a cue?

"Tracy, I've been thinking about Kevin Hewitt," he said.

"Oh, yes?"

"He's well-known to us, of course. And the funny thing is, I remember him. I even interviewed him a couple of times myself. But I never thought Hewitt was a real villain. He struck me as too much of a family man. He loved his kids, no doubt about it. I can't see him taking the risk of being put away and not seeing them for a few years."

"Things change," said Udall. "Children go through phases when they become unbearable. Sometimes I feel I wouldn't mind a spell in the nick to get away from *my* two. It'd be a nice holiday."

"I've watched my nieces grow up, but I suppose it's different when you're actually a parent."

"There's no escape," said Udall. "And a lot of men can't take that responsibility."

Cooper frowned thoughtfully. "Hewitt must know he's likely to land a prison sentence this time."

"Maybe he doesn't care any more, since his wife kicked him out. Some men get like that. They see themselves on the long slide downhill, and they can't face it. Then they turn reckless, as if they're inviting disaster. It's a sort of death wish."

"Rather prison than trying to live on your own?"

"Well, at least you have a place where you belong, a status in some kind of hierarchy, even if it's right at the bottom. It's an animal instinct, the desire to be part of a pack."

"And Kevin seems to know all about animal instincts."

Udall pulled her hat on and adjusted her belt. "It's true, though," she said. "We're not made to be solitary. Loneliness is the biggest killer there is."

Surprised, Cooper looked up at her. But she was already leaving.

By five-thirty, it was turning into a grey, claggy day, so common in the high moorland of the Dark

Peak. Cooper had crossed the viaduct over the drowned village of Ashopton, and turned off the A57 towards the Fairholmes visitor centre. Most of the pull-ins along the eastern arm of Ladybower Reservoir were full of cars, despite the weather.

On summer weekends, the road beyond Fairholmes was closed to traffic. A shuttle bus ran visitors up the valley instead, skirting the banks of the reservoirs as far as the turnaround at King's Tree. Occasionally, the police got calls from tourists who'd missed the last bus back and were too exhausted to face a six-mile walk.

Today, though, the road was open. Cooper steered cautiously through the ducks that waddled in ragged troupes across the road and drove through a gate past the western tower of Derwent Dam. In places, these reservoirs had formed sandy beaches that were exposed when the water level dropped. On a sunny day it was a bit like the seaside. Not quite the Costa del Sol, perhaps, but you could use your imagination.

It was only from the map that the geography of the Upper Derwent became clear. The long valley was filled with reservoirs — Howden, Derwent, Ladybower. The lower slopes were covered with conifer plantations, and above them rose the heather moorland, vast acres etched by cloughs and scattered with cairns. On some of those moors, there were no signs of civilisation for miles in any direction. Well, not unless you counted grouse butts as civilisation.

Cooper met Sergeant Jackson at a gate providing access on to Lightside Moor. He had another man with him, a middle aged figure in tweed cap, green shooting vest and brown corduroy trousers — an outfit designed to blend in with the moor. An English pointer sat behind him, constantly alert. Cooper approved of that. He liked a real working dog.

"This is Harry Blakelock, who owns Lightside," said Jackson. "Owner — and keeper too. Eh, Harry?"

"I just have a lad who helps me part-time," said Blakelock sourly. "There's not enough money in grouse shooting to employ full-time keepers. Not on a moor this size."

"Mr Blakelock says we can take my Landrover

most of the way across if we want," said Jackson. He raised an eyebrow. "But I thought you might rather walk."

"Suits me."

Cooper laced his boots and fastened his leggings. With a woolly hat, he'd be indistinguishable from any walker on the moors. Blakelock watched him, his jowly cheeks sunk into the collar of his jacket. Cooper noticed a green gun slip on the ground nearby, the carrying case for Blakelock's shotgun. He'd almost missed seeing it in the heather, and he knew it wasn't approved practice to leave a gun lying around, even for a few minutes. But Mr Blakelock wouldn't have been shooting at this time of year, unless he was taking crows and pigeons. They were classed as pests, and therefore open season.

"Stay on the paths," said Blakelock. "Don't go disturbing my birds."

Jackson nodded. "Don't worry, Harry."

Cooper gave the moor owner a smile, which wasn't returned. The birds that concerned Blakelock were red grouse. They'd be his source of income once the shooting season started next month.

At first glance, Lightside Moor seemed almost featureless, the banks of heather and whinberry blurring into the distance. As they headed up the first slope, Cooper caught a glimpse of something yellow below the crest of a ridge, but within a couple of steps it was hidden by the terrain.

Cooper looked at the map for the names of the moors. He saw Alport, Westend, Ronksley. And this one, Lightside, surrounded on all sides by more moorland, plantations to the east, and the boggy ground of Featherbed Moss to the north. Gamekeepers tended these moors all year, battling encroaching vegetation and disease-carrying ticks. And, of course, the predators — or 'vermin', as so many keepers called them.

"So where do you think the biggest risks for birds of prey come from, Sergeant?" he asked, pausing to let the older man catch up.

"Well, pigeon fanciers don't like them — particularly peregrines, because they take racing pigeons sometimes. And gamekeepers don't like any birds of prey, because they think they reduce the grouse population."

"Well, they do. Don't they?"

Jackson's breath was getting ragged as they approached the top of the moor. "Some do. Hen harriers."

"Anyone else?"

"Oh, a few serial egg collectors are still out there. And raptor keepers who want to improve a captive strain."

They came across a grouse butt that had been dug into a peat bank and shored up with sheets of corrugated iron. On the next slope, Cooper could see another butt. And beyond that a third, and a fourth.

The yellow shape he'd glimpsed turned out to be a battered fibreglass shelter. The foam insulation was peeling from the walls, and swallows had built their nest in a loose fold of foam. Two scarred wooden benches inside could probably seat about ten men with their guns and dogs when the weather turned bad during a shoot. But visitors other than shooters had engraved disrespectful graffiti in the remaining insulation.

In the valley behind him, Cooper saw Howden

Reservoir, sheltering deep in its conifer plantations. The only sounds on the moor were curlew and snipe, crying at the presence of intruders.

"Nearly there now," said Jackson. "Thank God."

It looked like an ordinary garden shed. A shed that someone had dropped from an aircraft on to a remote part of the moors. Okay, they'd dropped it carefully — it was perfectly intact, anchored to the ground and coated with preservative. Its weather boarding and green felt roof looked incongruous above the crags of Alport Castles, though. It was one of the most unlikely tourist attractions Cooper could imagine, even in the Peak District. This was where people came to watch birds displaying over the crags.

"We might see birds here, if we're lucky," said Jackson.

Cooper had brought his own binoculars, an old pair of Zeiss 10 × 50s. He adjusted them as Jackson explained the excitement about eggs being laid in goshawk nests since late April. Incubation lasted for around five weeks, and that was the time when nest sites attracted the attention of predators in human shape. Egg collectors wanted freshly laid eggs, which were easier to blow, so they were out in their camouflage gear as soon as word got round that the first goshawk was laying.

"They spend all winter planning their next season, as if it's a military campaign — targets, tactics, how to avoid the enemy," said Jackson. "They're really getting organised."

Alport Castles themselves towered over the valley and the farmstead way below. Tors perched precariously on the summit, and boulders were tumbled on the slopes. If the mist descended, it would be easy to look out of the corners of your eyes and mistake the thousands of gritstone boulders for the shapes of people, crowds of them standing perfectly still and ghost-like on the edge of the moor.

Cooper noticed a pair of black shapes circling over the moor, and turned his binoculars westwards. Carrion crows. This pair probablythey had their eyes on a weak lamb somewhere. Soon they'd land nearby and wait for it to weaken.

Then they'd begin to work on its eyes, like delicacies that had to be eaten fresh. Once their victim was blinded, the crows could eat the rest of it at their leisure.

"And what if the goshawk's eggs survive to be hatched?"

"Then the egg collectors are replaced by people who want live chicks to sell, or to raise in captivity. It's a never-ending battle, Ben."

Cooper tried to analyse the background noise. He couldn't see a road from here, so probably it was only the sound of the wind scything through the plantations. Close to the edge, the gusts were dangerously strong, banging angrily between the rocks. A half-grown sheep called plaintively — a strange, unnatural cry that stuck in its throat.

He lifted the binoculars again, and saw a single outline soaring over the valley. This time, it was a peregrine. The bird rose effortlessly on a thermal, then flicked a wing and swooped behind the crags, perhaps spotting the movement of prey.

"*They* don't need binoculars," said Jackson.

Watching the bird, Cooper found the phrase 'eagle eyed' going through his mind. The only way the police could achieve that sort of surveillance in the Upper Derwent was to get Oscar Hotel 88 airborne from Ripley, and there was no way he could justify the cost of a helicopter.

"It's amazing there are still individuals plundering nests," said Jackson. "They obviously haven't heard about the measures we're taking to protect endangered species these days."

"They might have done," said Cooper. "Publicity doesn't necessarily deter people. They always think it can't happen to them."

"Well, the last one was caught by the cameras. He wasn't too difficult to identify, because he was a known collector."

"I've heard you sometimes use off-duty police officers pretending to be campers," said Cooper. "Is that right?"

Jackson smiled. "I believe it is."

In fact, Cooper knew an officer who'd volunteered for the job, and had spent three days in the Upper Derwent with his tent and binoculars. A few hours of your time were worthwhile if you cared about the national park's wildlife. Maybe that was what Sergeant Jackson had in mind for him.

Cooper noticed a figure striding purposefully towards them along the edge of the moor.

"Who's this?"

"Oh, it's one of our volunteers," said Jackson. "A keen birdwatcher, Calvin Ryan. And when I say keen — ."

"He'd have to be really dedicated to come all the way up here."

"Oh, he's here regularly. Cal is a bit of a crank, I suppose, but we can't discourage him. The more eyes we have, the better."

Ryan was wearing a knitted beanie hat, pulled so low that it almost met his goatee beard. His rucksack had pockets and Velcro straps that held camera, notebook, mobile phone, and other items that Tracy Udall might have been happy to wear on her belt.

"Peregrine," he said, gesturing excitedly.

"Yes, we've seen it."

Ryan wiped a sheen of sweat from his forehead with the back of a hand, and looked at Cooper. "Peregrines were almost wiped out in Derbyshire, thanks to pesticides. When they came back, Alport Castles was the first site they chose to begin breeding again."

"This is one of my colleagues, Cal," said Jackson. "He's not a tourist."

Ryan looked disappointed. "Oh."

But he wasn't deterred for long from expressing his enthusiasm. He followed the flight of the bird over the valley with eagerness.

"I love the goshawks and peregrines," he said. "They're the most fantastic of all the birds."

"They look great when they're flying," agreed Cooper.

"It's not just the way they look."

Ryan laid a hand on his sleeve, gripping a bit too tightly. "Goshawks mate for life, you know. A bonded pair will hunt co-operatively, two of them together. Then, when the chicks are hatched, the tercel isn't allowed near the nest. He has to leave the food he catches at a distance, where the female bird can fetch it for the chicks."

They lost sight of the bird again, and a moment of silence followed, as if they'd just been deprived of their reason for communicating with each other.

"Do they fly a long way from the nest site?"

asked Cooper.

"The male hunts up to three miles away."

"So anyone with a rifle could pick off that bird, and we'd never be any wiser."

"That's what happened in the past, we think," said Jackson. "The male birds just disappeared. If they were killed, the bodies were either removed by someone, or eaten by scavengers."

Ryan tugged angrily at his hat. "Not this one. He'll be back. Sometimes when he catches prey, he stores it in a safe place for feeding on later."

"I suppose a little bit of decay makes the meat tastier," suggested Jackson. "It's like you'd hang a joint of beef for a few days to make it sweet and tender."

Ryan pulled a disgusted expression. "I'd like you to know I'm a vegetarian."

A gust of wind blew along the edge of the valley, and a shower spattered their faces.

"We need more people watching," said Ryan. "More eyes equals more protection."

"So I heard."

Yes, Cooper had heard it from Phil Jackson

only a few minutes earlier, but not with so much fervour.

"Look at this place," said Ryan, waving a dismissive hand at the grouse moor behind him. "Birds that hunt the moorland are persecuted so much they've stopped breeding altogether in prime habitats."

Cooper glanced at Jackson, but he was edging away, on the pretence of checking the moorings of the shed.

"So you blame the moorland owners and gamekeepers, Mr Ryan?"

Ryan glared at him as if Cooper had just called his entire belief system into doubt.

"Persecution definitely exists," he said. "You can see that. And these grouse moors are where the conflict occurs."

"The problem comes from a minority, though, surely? There are people who actively protect birds of prey, but also shoot."

Ryan seemed to hold himself in with an effort. "I don't have a problem with shooting. But I do have a problem with raptor persecution. The bottom line is that birds of prey are protected by law."

Ryan hitched his rucksack and moved off along the edge, with the air of someone who'd won an argument through sheer righteousness. He reminded Cooper of a street preacher — one of those wild-eyed men who lurked outside shopping precincts, confident that they only had to shout at people long enough for everyone to agree with them.

Jackson smiled at Cooper when Ryan was out of earshot.

"Cal's right, though," he said. "At the end of the day, it was public opinion that led to a ban on fox hunting. What will be next on the public's list of things to ban if they see birds of prey being killed?"

"You think the shooters and shoot owners are worried?"

For a moment, Jackson followed the flight of the peregrine until it vanished against the background of heather.

"I think some of them will be panicking," he said. "There's a propaganda war going on, Ben — and they're losing right now."

* * *

The next tree was even higher. Hewitt had to lean against the trunk for a while until he felt strong enough to carry on. He dug a bottle of water out of his pocket and took a long drink, then urinated on the grass at the base of the fir. It was supposed to bring good luck, wasn't it?

Hewitt grinned to himself, but the sweat drying on his face made smiling uncomfortable. What he really needed was a nice stream nearby. He could imagine clear, cold water tumbling over a few stones, tinged slightly brown from the peat, like a good malt whisky. Water was everywhere in the Peak District, cascading in torrents from the hills to fill up the reservoirs. But there was no stream here in the plantation. Not for half a mile or so, way back across the moor.

Then Hewitt saw the bird. It swooped over the woods, hovered for a second, then soared out again, far above his head. He caught the flicker of plumage and saw the shape of the wings against the light as it turned. A goshawk. Probably the male bird, the tercel, hunting for prey to feed its mate and the chicks in the nest.

Fumbling for his binoculars, Hewitt moved away from the tree and tried to keep the bird in sight. If it decided to pursue something on the ground, it would move too fast for him to follow. But if he could track its movements and see where it returned to, it would save him a lot of pain and effort.

He lost the goshawk for a moment, and scanned backwards and forwards over the moor anxiously, straining his eyes to pick out any movement against the background. He caught up with the bird as it skimmed low over a slope. It was swinging its head from side to side, searching for rodents in the vegetation. Hewitt admired the grace of its flight, the way it hardly seemed to move its wings to maintain height, just that flick of a pinion to change direction or catch a thermal and rise several feet in a second.

And then he heard the shot. The crack of it echoed across the moor and into the valley, bouncing of the ramparts of Alport Castles.

And suddenly the bird was gone from his field of vision. Hewitt was left with nothing more than the impression of exploding feathers, a body that was lighter than air tossed over and over, like a rag caught in the wind. Somebody had shot the tercel.

3.

Next morning, Sergeant Jackson came into the CID office at Edendale. He was carrying an evidence bag that contained a dead goshawk.

"A walker picked it up, and phoned in," he said. "Another few hours, and the carcass would have disappeared, one way or another."

"Shot?"

"Yes."

Cooper watched Jackson turn the bird over in his hands, examining its wings, the talons and beak — all the hallmarks of a raptor. There was even a reason why its legs and feet were bare of feathers. It was so they didn't get covered in blood when it sank its talons into prey.

But there was blood now, and plenty of it — the whole of the bird's left side was matted.

Cooper could sense Jackson's despair at the fate of the goshawk. Almost the only action he could take was to record the incident. And even that was a recent innovation. For many years, no police force had prioritised wildlife incidents, because they weren't recordable. If you cleared up a burglary, it came off the crime figures. But catch a bird thief, and it didn't show up in any statistics. No target to be met, no performance to be measured. Now at least the public could see that offences were being dealt with.

Beyond that, Jackson's options were limited. It wasn't like a burglary, where there might be witnesses, fingerprints, a car registration to follow up. Wildlife crime happened in remote areas, on private land. Not much chance of a witness, and no forensic evidence. Even if you had a suspect, it would be someone with a legitimate reason to be at the scene. After the introduction of Right to Roam legislation, that meant pretty much everyone.

"It's very frustrating," said Jackson. "So many wildlife criminals are involved in other offences. Arrest one, and you collar a well-known villain."

"But what are your chances of an arrest?"

"Zero."

Cooper felt strangely relieved when Jackson took the goshawk away. There was always something alien about a dead bird. It was probably that third eyelid, the nictating membrane, that closed from the inside corner to protect the eye. It was so reptilian that it marked birds as survivors from an earlier age.

"Well, I think it's definitely a sadistic offence," said Udall when she heard the news. "These are people who take pleasure in inflicting cruelty. They're potential serial killers."

"That's putting it a bit strong, Tracy."

"Don't psychologists say the typical serial killer starts his careers by mistreating animals? It's part of the pattern."

"Yes, they do say that."

"After all, this is someone who's prepared to use violence on a casual basis. If he lacks respect for animal life, he might not respect human life, either."

Half an hour later, Cooper's phone rang. It was Sergeant Jackson again.

"Maybe not zero after all," he said. "Cal Ryan says he was up at the hide when the goshawk was shot."

"Did he see anything?"

"Yes. He saw Harry Blakelock. And Mr Blakelock was carrying a firearm."

"I'll have to talk to him, Phil. Is that okay with you?"

"You're the detective." Jackson sounded bitter. But a moment later, his tone changed. "No, that's fine. I might still have to work with the man when this is over."

"I'll get up there today. He lives at Lightside Lodge, doesn't he?"

"Yes. But he'll be out on the moor on a day like this. I can give you his mobile number so you can track him down."

"Thanks, Phil."

"There's another thing. A whole bunch of twitchers were down in the valley at the time. You often see them lined up near Derwent Dam with their telescopes and telephoto lenses. One or two of them have helped us in the past. And they're famil-iar with the major egg collectors. Word goes round the bird watching community like wildfire."

"You mean they saw Hewitt?"

"No, Gareth Stark. Every clued-up twitcher knows about Stark. They were breaking out the champagne when he went down."

"Don't tell me Stark was spotted in the valley when the bird was shot, too?"

"No. But his car was."

"That complicates the picture," said Cooper.

"Do you want me to speak to Stark?"

"Would you, Phil?"

"With pleasure."

"I'll ask Tracy Udall if she'd like to come along. If Stark calls her 'my dear' once more —."

Jackson laughed. "Tell her she'll be welcome. I'm getting a bit slow on my feet these days, and I might not be able to hold her back."

Harry Blakelock was carrying a twelve-bore side-lock with a thirty-inch barrel. When Cooper got a closer look, he could see that it was a magnificent Purdey, with beautiful engravings. It must have been worth fifteen thousand pounds at least, even second hand. He knew from the firearms licensing records that Mr Blakelock had a safe somewhere at home, with at least three more shotguns in it.

As Cooper approached, Blakelock's English pointer was creeping across a stretch of boggy ground, her body rigid from nose to tail. She'd detected the scent of grouse hiding in the heather.

"That's Molly," said Blakelock. "Useful dog."

"I have a few questions to ask you, sir."

"Go ahead, then."

Blakelock listened in stony silence to Cooper's questions. Then he slapped the stock of his gun.

"I was up here on the moor, as you know damn well. You saw me yourself. But I was back home by six-thirty, and I went nowhere near those woods. You can check my gun over, if you want. I shot a crow a few minutes ago, and there's still a cartridge in."

"It won't tell me anything."

"Of course it won't."

A covey of grouse broke cover, flapping furiously to escape. But they were in luck today. Blakelock was only checking how many birds there were, not intending to deplete their numbers. It was over a month yet before the grouse season started, and these birds would begin to plummet out of the sky. Cooper knew real shooters were scornful of the rush to be the first to kill a bird on the opening day of the season. The Glorious Twelfth was just a marketing ploy, they said, a photo opportunity for the media. But proper shooting would follow soon after, grouse being driven by beaters towards paying guns.

As the squawking birds gained speed and altitude, Molly was already pointing out another covey in the heather. Blakelock turned to watch her.

"I know your brother, don't I?" he said over his shoulder. "Matt Cooper? He has a farm near Hucklow."

"That's right."

"And I remember your grandfather — he was a grand old bloke. And wasn't your father — ?"

"Yes, I'm sure you knew him, too."

"Well, you must know the way it is — these bird groups have got to increase their membership, so they put out sensationalist reports. They quote incidents which are just plain bloody wrong. They don't know who's causing the problem, so it must be gamekeepers. But I've seen reports that disturbance by bird watchers is responsible for the loss of birds. The tercel sees a crowd of twitchers near his nest, and he says 'sod this, I'm off'."

Cooper was getting irritated by the clouds of black flies dancing over the heather. They were always a problem on a warm, still day.

"There are always two sides, Mr Blakelock," he said.

"Come off it. These bird groups, they're completely blinkered. They don't care about the wider picture. Without shoots, these moors would be abandoned to the damn dog owners, and the ramblers. There'd be no wildlife up here, that's for sure. And there's a demand for shooting, you know. Not just in this country — I have a party of Germans who book a few days on the moor every year. Businessmen from Frankfurt."

"You know that some people would question

the morality of shooting wildlife for pleasure?"

"Pleasure?" said Blakelock. "I get pleasure from the skill it takes to put the grouse here in the first place. I get pleasure from the surroundings I spend time in. And from the co-ordination of hand and eye, if you like. But not from the act of killing."

"But most of the killing is done by people who pay money to do it."

"If a hundred grouse need culling, why should I do it myself when there are people willing to pay? Anyway, we try to be selective on our shoots. If you've got a seasoned eye, you can pick out the oldest bird in a covey as they scatter. I don't allow massacres."

"Is it always so straightforward?"

Blakelock didn't answer the question directly. He broke the shotgun open, emptied the remaining cartridge, and put the gun away in its slip.

"There's this idea some people have of putting an end to shooting and returning the moors to their original state," he said. "It's completely impractical, you know. The balance of nature was altered centuries ago."

"And, as you said, the grouse bring in money."

"A day's shooting might bring in eight thousand pounds or so. But the money gets paid straight back out to keepers and beaters. Nobody's getting rich owning a grouse moor."

"Then why spend so much effort destroying the predators?"

Blakelock looked at him coolly. "All your family have been shooters, Detective Constable Cooper. I bet you've even been on shoots yourself, haven't you? Local farmers and their families often get invited for a day out on the moor."

The staccato warning call of a grouse rattled across the moors. *Go back, go back, go back.* Cooper wafted the flies from his face, trying to gain time before he answered.

"Yes, I know a bit about shooting."

"Bagged a few grouse yourself, I dare say?"

"I stick to clays these days, Mr Blakelock."

Blakelock called his dog to heel. "I really don't understand it. You're shooting people, all you Coopers. You always have been. Yet here you are, harrassing people like me, just because I'm going about my legitimate business. Very odd. Give someone a uniform and a warrant card, and suddenly they forget which side they're on."

"I'm not on anyone's side, sir. My job is to see the law doesn't get broken."

"Sometimes, when there are bad laws, you have to choose," said Blakelock. "Those are the times when we all have to take sides."

"Stark had an alibi," said Udall, the moment Cooper returned to the office in Edendale. "Bastard."

"But his car was identified, wasn't it? According to Phil Jackson, the twitchers even took his licence number."

"Oh, he was in the valley all right. But he was with a woman. Can you believe it?"

Cooper laughed at her expression. "It takes all sorts, Tracy."

"They went to Fairholmes for a picnic, then hired a couple of bikes for a romantic ride along Derwent Reservoir. She corroborates his story in full. We've even got his signature in the book at the hire centre. Stark had the nerve to tell us that he was paying a nostalgic visit to old haunts."

"Did you believe him?"

"No, I didn't. To be honest, I was amazed when I found it really was a woman he was with. I was pretty sure it was you he fancied in that interview room, not me."

"For heaven's sake, Tracy —."

"Oh, sod it. You never heard me say that."

Cooper watched her fiddling with her belt, tugging at it as if the thing was never going to be comfortable, no matter what she did. When Udall stood close to his desk, he could smell the familiar aroma of wool and polyester. Police uniform trousers. They were notoriously ill-fitting and itchy to wear, too.

"Have you any idea how many twitchers were in the valley that day, Tracy?"

"Fifty, sixty. Why?"

"You know, some of the shooting fraternity argue that it's disturbance by bird watchers that scares the goshawks off."

Udall sucked her teeth. "Perhaps."

"They've got a point, when you see the crowds of twitchers lined up with their binoculars and telephoto lenses."

"I said 'perhaps'."

Cooper picked up a file that had been left on his desk and read the first page. "Did you know that Harry Blakelock once had his firearms certificate revoked?"

"Oh? A security breach? Or a domestic?"

"Neither," said Cooper.

He turned the file over to the reasons for revocation. Many cases like this cropped up each year, some of them stupid and unavoidable. They mostly involved insecure storage — guns abandoned in a Landrover outside a pub, or even in a field after a shoot. Of course, people who didn't know any better shouldn't be allowed to own a gun.

But there were also an increasing number of domestic incidents. A certificate holder could be vulnerable to complaints by his partner that he'd made threats. Cooper knew of one man who'd lost his firearms certificate on a drink driving conviction. But this case wasn't any of those.

"It appears Mr Blakelock went to his GP and asked for an anti-depressant prescription," he said. "Grounds for revocation: a mental illness, meaning that he can't possess firearms without being a potential danger to the public"

"Damn," said Udall. "I bet that really pissed him off."

"The lesson is not to be in too much of a hurry to talk to your doctor, I suppose."

"But he must have got his certificate back?"

Cooper remembered the Purdey. "Oh, surely."

It was recorded in the file that Blakelock had found a solicitor in East Anglia who specialised in shooting law, and he'd lodged a successful appeal against revocation.

"I've heard the name of this solicitor before," said Cooper. "He handles a lot of Firearms Act appeals."

"Part of the preventative justice system, then. Balancing the public interest against an individual's right to possess a gun."

Cooper shrugged. "He did a good job for Mr Blakelock."

"Hoorah for justice."

It was a shame to be so cynical so young, but Cooper knew he couldn't judge Udall when his life experience was so different from hers. While she was listening to a burst of chatter from her radio, he picked up another file that had been left for him.

"Now this is interesting, Tracy. Kevin Hewitt's phone records."

"Anything of significance?"

"Mostly calls to his wife. Some long conversations — chatting to the kids, probably. A couple of calls to Gareth Stark. We'll have to ask him about those. But get this, Tracy — there have been three calls made to Lightside Lodge. That's Harry Blakelock's number."

Udall pursed her lips. "What's the connection between those two?"

"I don't know. But —."

But she was listening to her radio again, and Cooper realised he'd lost her attention.

"They've found Hewitt's Bedford van," she said. "Parked by the Westend River bridge."

"On the banks of Howden?"

"That's the place."

The van didn't take long to open. In the back, they found a pair of aluminium climbing irons fitted with fibreglass shin guards and Velcro straps.

"Geckos," said Cooper, touching a finger to the flat tips of the gaffs. "There's a couple of hundred pounds in these irons alone. But Kevin Hewitt has been unemployed for months. He's been getting money from somewhere, all right."

There was also a pair of climbing gloves, spare boots, a rucksack, and a set of plastic boxes like those in Hewitt's trophy room. Udall had found a rolled sleeping bag and a blanket. She turned out the contents of the rucksack, and pulled her face at the smell of dirty clothes.

"That answers the question of where he's been sleeping since we raided his council house. He couldn't go back to his wife, since she decided she didn't like living with a criminal and kicked him out. So Kevin's been living in his van."

Cooper lifted a digital camera out of the glove compartment. "I don't believe Janine Hewitt kicked her husband out because he was a criminal. It was because she was frightened he'd get caught. She didn't want her children coming into contact with the police and Social Services."

"I can relate to that."

"On the other hand, I think she would certainly be reluctant to give up benefiting from the proceeds of Kevin's activities."

"So they'd have had to get together and find a way for Kevin to pass the money on without going to the house. I can understand that, from her point of view. But why would Kevin take the risk? What was in it for him?"

"It was his only chance of staying in touch with his kids," said Cooper. "Whatever else Kevin Hewitt's faults are, I think he loves his children."

Udall straightened up. "Well, there's no hoard of cash in this van, any more than there was in his house. So where's Kevin now?"

Cooper looked at the conifer plantations surrounding the reservoirs, and the vast expanses of moorland beyond them.

"I don't know. But I'm getting a really bad feeling about Kevin Hewitt's future."

Janine Hewitt was wearing a completely impractical pair of shoes in the park that day. They were red and strappy, with heels that wobbled when she stood up to check on the child in the pushchair.

"I bought these on eBay," she said, when she saw Cooper looking at them. "They were only a fiver."

Cooper wondered if he was supposed to compliment her on her taste. But a glance at Janine's expression told him that she didn't expect anything. No compliments, no sympathy. Not from him, not from anybody.

"How are the children?"

"They're all right," she said listlessly. "I'll be glad when they're all at school. But I suppose it could be worse."

"Worse?"

"There are only two of them," she said. "Some women round here, they have a house full by the time they're thirty. Poor cows."

For the first time, Cooper noticed how pale and weary she looked. He wondered if she was ill, or whether it was just exhaustion, the day to day grind of bringing up young children on her own. He knew there couldn't be much money in the household. A fiver on a pair of shoes was an extravagance, intended only to raise her spirits for a short while.

"Janine, your husband could be in danger, did you know that?"

She looked up at him. "Could he?"

"We think so."

She gazed across the park, tears suddenly glistening in her eyes, as if emotion had sneaked up on her unexpectedly. Cooper looked away, embarrassed. Talking to Janine Hewitt made him wonder about this whole mating for life thing. All that pairing, breeding, and caring for the young. Then watching them learn to fly and fend for themselves. And doing it all over again the next year.

"Kevin was okay until they got their claws into him," she said suddenly.

"They? Who are 'they'?"

"There were a couple of foreigners," she said. "Kevin said they were Germans, who came over here looking for birds."

"Falconers?"

"I don't know what that means. They wanted birds to train for hunting. Kevin said they'd pay good money for the right bird. That's what every-one wants these days, not eggs."

"Yes. He was talking about falconers."

"Did he mention any names, Janine?" asked Udall. "Or where he met them?"

"He never told me anything like that. I didn't know any details, and I didn't ask. It's best not to know. That's what Kevin always said."

"Sometimes it's true."

Janine found a tissue and wiped her eyes. "You know, I told Kevin if he could get us out of this place, I'd have him back."

"Get you out?"

"Find us a proper home, somewhere nice. Not this shit hole. I want a house of my own, a garden the kids can play in. I'm not going to stay living next door to a bunch of drug addicts who leave the yard full of syringes for Jack to pick up. I can't have my kids sleeping in rooms so damp the wall-paper won't stay on the walls. I want to get right out of the Devonshire Estate."

"How would Kevin find enough money for that?" asked Cooper.

"There are ways," she said. "Everyone knows

there are ways to get money. Look at some of the people round here. Do you think they live on a few quid a week in child benefit, like I do?"

"Janine — are you telling us you put pressure on Kevin to commit more and more serious crimes? You actually encouraged him to get in deeper?"

She'd begun to cry again. The child in the pushchair turned to look, stirred out of her apathy by the sound of her mother sobbing.

"No, no. I didn't do that."

"Well, that's what happened, Janine. Isn't it?"

"I never seriously thought there was a chance he'd get enough money together. Not Kevin."

"You underestimated him, then."

Janine laughed through the tears. "Hardly. I've never seen anything from him. And I don't suppose I will now."

"You haven't seen anything? No money?"

"No. He promised me he'd do it one day. But, like I said, he never got it together. That was Kevin all over."

Cooper and Udall looked at each other. They knew that Kevin Hewitt had found at least one source of money. So what happened to it?

"Germans?" said Cooper when they were back in the car. "I can't believe she said Germans. An international connection is all we need, Tracy."

"Our wildlife officers have contact with their counterparts in Europe," said Udall. "German falconers are often mentioned in their intelligence reports. They roam the whole of Europe in search of new material, even as far as Greenland to obtain gyr falcons. I'm told falconry is very popular in Germany."

"Don't they breed their own chicks?"

"Some falconers do. But not on a large enough scale to meet the demand."

"And, in this case, the demand is for young birds."

"Yes. Young enough to be trained."

"Why does everything come down to supply and demand, Tracy?"

"It's what makes the world go round."

Cooper gazed at the Devonshire Estate as they drove down the street. Some of the addresses in this area were the homes of the most active drug dealers in town — people who certainly lived much better than Janine Hewitt.

"Harry Blakelock mentioned a party of Germans who book a few days on his grouse shoot every year," he said. "He said they were business-men from Frankfurt."

"Maybe they are."

Cooper felt easier as the outlines of the hills became visible beyond the streets of the estate. "You know, I bet Mr Blakelock would do any-thing to avoid losing his shotgun licence again. He'd stand no chance of winning an appeal a second time, no matter how good a lawyer he got."

"So if someone had a bit of information about him — ? Information they might be inclined to report to the police, which could lose him his cer-tificate."

"Yes. Anything might do it, too — evidence of a security breach, an assault, drunk driving. Another medical problem."

"He'd want to keep them quiet somehow."

Cooper nodded. "Despite his complaints, Blakelock must have plenty of money. He'd be a prime target for blackmail, wouldn't you say?"

"A sitting duck."

Cooper sighted along the barrels, shifted his grip on the stock and breathed in the scent of gun oil as his fingers felt for the trigger. The shotgun fitted snugly into his shoulder, and the weight of the double barrels swung smoothly as he turned his body. With that movement came an eagerness to see the target in his sights, a desire for the kick and cough of the cartridge. He was ready.

"Pull!"

The launcher snapped and a clay flashed across his line of vision. The barrels swung up and to the right to follow its trajectory, and his finger squeezed. The clay shattered into fragments that curved towards the ground.

"Pull!"

The second clay flickered overhead. Cooper carefully increased the pressure on the trigger, timing the extra squeeze as the target's line steadied. The clay shattered like the first.

"Nice," he said, breaking the shotgun open as his brother Matt walked across from the trap.

"That Remington's a well-made piece of equipment, isn't it?" said Matt.

"The best."

It was the gun Cooper had won the Shooting Trophy with a couple of years ago, but he hardly had time for it these days, not since he'd moved out of the farm. The residents of Welbeck Street wouldn't be quite so relaxed about him carrying a shotgun around.

In addition to the trap, Matt had brought out three boxes of clay pigeons and a hundred cartridges. The small black pellets in those cartridges were enough to smash a clay. But when they caught a real bird in their lethal hail, they pierced its flesh and lodged in its muscles and internal organs, maybe in its brain. Cooper supposed it was a quick death.

"I've just bought a new gun," said Matt. "A Baikal Choke. I paid £400 for it."

"A bargain."

And probably it was. But a £400 Baikal was a bit different from Harry Blakelock's Purdey. And a clay pigeon was a different prospect from a grouse on Lightside Moor, too. Grouse were so attractive because they were uniquely difficult to shoot. It was impossible to simulate their speed, their style of flight, or the way they sprang up from the heather anywhere, even from behind you. No set of clays could match that.

Cooper knew some people saw grouse shooting as an anachronism — they pictured the tweed-clad rich blasting away at wildlife, like a scene from some nineteenth century novel. Others were uneasy about deriving pleasure from the destruction of living creatures. Killing an animal was one thing. When it had to be done, there was a satisfaction in knowing you'd done the job properly.

He turned away to put his shotgun in the Land Rover, where he locked it into a steel box. But getting pleasure from killing? Yes, he had to agree. That was a different thing altogether.

4.

By Friday, Kevin Hewitt lay on a stainless steel table. Entering the mortuary, Cooper could see that his egg collecting career was at an end. Janine's children were without a father.

He wondered whether Jack and Ebony would mourn their dad and remember him forever, or forget him within a few months. Maybe Janine would introduce another man into their lives and tell them he was their new dad. Unlike goshawks, people didn't necessarily mate for life.

"A heart attack?" asked Cooper. "Or did he just lose his grip and fall?"

The pathologist, Doctor Juliana van Doon, pulled down her mask and drew off her latex gloves.

"Well, your deceased certainly fell, DC Cooper. It was the force of his impact with the ground that killed him. There are multiple internal injuries — all listed in my report, if you need them. But his heart wasn't in good condition, either. How did you know that?"

"It was just a guess, ma'am."

Mrs van Doon smiled. "Well, there's a lot of fatty degeneration present, which would have been dangerous at his age — especially if he was in the habit of climbing trees. Some people never learn how to adapt their lifestyles to their physical capabilities. But Mr Hewitt didn't live long enough to experience a heart attack."

"What do you mean?"

"I suspect *this* was what made him fall."

Cooper realised the pathologist was holding a stainless steel bowl. At the bottom was a tiny, black metal ball that was almost invisible against the gleam of the metal, but rattled ominously when she tipped the bowl.

"An airgun pellet," he said.

"That's what I thought. But I'm glad to hear

you confirm it."

"Where did you find it?"

Mrs van Doon pointed with her scalpel. "I removed the pellet from a wound in the deceased's scalp, just behind the right ear. The entry wound was almost masked by a contusion from the fall — that's why it wasn't evident at the preliminary examination."

"Could it be left over from an old injury? These things are so tiny — they can stay in the body for years without the victim being aware of them."

"No, the wound was fresh. The track of the pellet into the flesh is still clear, and there was no sign of healing."

"So he was shot with an air rifle while he was in the tree," said Cooper.

"That's what it looks like."

Cooper didn't feel convinced. Unlike a shotgun, an airgun fired a single lead pellet. It was useful for controlling pest species, provided they could be shot at short distances, thirty-five yards or less. And there had been plenty of people who'd lost an eye in a close-range accident. But an airgun pellet wouldn't normally kill a human being.

"No, the pellet wouldn't have caused a serious injury in itself," said Mrs van Doon when he mentioned it. "But it would have given Mr Hewitt quite a shock. There would certainly be a sharp pain. I imagine you'd instinctively put a hand up to the place you were hit."

"And that was enough for him to lose his grip."

"Yes, I'd say so. If you like, we could start calling him 'the victim' now, instead of 'the deceased'."

Cooper looked at the pellet again. "For all Kevin Hewitt knew, he might have been stung by a wasp or something. If he never saw the shooter, he wouldn't have been able to tell the difference."

"Yes, I'm sure you're right. The pellet would have come right out of the blue." Mrs Van Doon shook the dish again. "So there you have it, DC Cooper — here's a case where you could say the victim literally didn't know what hit him."

Tracy Udall pulled up a chair in the CID room, ignoring the stares of the other detectives. Cooper had asked her to help him go over the evidence, to try to make sense of Kevin Hewitt's last few weeks of life.

"Well, let's look for a motive. Who might have had it for Kevin?"

"Gareth Stark, definitely," said Udall. "He has a grudge against Hewitt for his conviction. And the Germans — I bet they want the money back they paid for a goshawk."

"Okay. And Harry Blakelock?"

"Yes, if Hewitt had something on him."

Cooper looked up. "Tracy, were there any photographs found in Hewitt's house?"

"No, but there was a digital camera in the van, with a spare memory stick."

"So there was."

"Judging by his meticulous filing, I suppose he must have taken photos to record his finds, too."

"Have we looked what's on the camera?"

"Not yet. Well, it didn't seem important. It'll just be eggs, Ben."

"Retrieve it from Exhibits, will you? And the memory stick, too."

Udall returned a few minutes later with the camera, and connected it up to a PC. There were lots of photos. And Tracy was right, most of them were of eggs. There was also an entire sequence showing the acquisition of the goshawk chick — the nestling still in its nest, the young chick in its cage at Hewitt's house.

But right in the middle of the sequence, there were some shots Cooper couldn't make out at first. They had been taken from some high vantage point, possibly in the very tree Hewitt had found the nest. Shots of Harry Blakelock, and a gun left unattended on the moor. The time stamp from the camera was evidence of how long the gun was left before its owner returned.

"Blackmail material," said Udall.

"I wonder how much Hewitt was asking for it."

"Too much for Blakelock to stomach?"

Cooper sighed. "So Kevin Hewitt not only upset bird enthusiasts, but his former partner, a bunch of Germans, the local drug dealers, and even Harry Blakelock. He pissed everyone off. That's quite an achievement."

"Not forgetting his wife," said Udall.

"Janine?"

"Possibly the most unforgiving of all."

"You're right." Cooper tapped his pen thoughtfully. "Tracy, what would you have done if you'd been in Hewitt's position?"

"I'd have kept my head down. Left the area, probably. But, as Janine said, someone had their claws into him. Kevin was driven by more than a concern for his own popularity."

Cooper thought about Hewitt's home circumstances. He still believed he'd been right in his original assessment of the man. Kevin Hewitt didn't need to have anyone's claws sunk into him, when he was already wriggling on the painful hook of family, the sharp barbs sunk into his flesh by a love for his children. He wasn't the sort of man to slip free from that responsibility.

"Anything else?" asked Udall, as if she thought he'd nodded off.

"Yes. Ballistics say the airgun pellet was a .22. Probably something like Vermin Pell."

"Vermin Pell? What a lovely name."

"It's self explanatory," said Cooper. "They're designed for taking out vermin."

Udall looked at him as if he'd said something inappropriate.

"I'm not suggesting that Kevin Hewitt —."

"I know, Ben." She turned over a page of the file. "And I see that Hewitt's clothes were marked with Smart Water. He'd found the right tree, then."

"Yes."

Smart Water. Another high-tech weapon in Peak Nestwatch's armoury — a chemical treatment sprayed on trees at a height where it could only be picked up by climbing. A suspect's clothes could be examined under ultra-violet light, to prove whether he'd climbed that specific tree.

Cooper stared at Udall, suddenly aware of something glaringly obvious that he'd overlooked.

"I'm being an idiot," he said. "It should have been the first action we took."

"Oh?" Udall frowned. "I'm not with you. You mean, if Hewitt's killer touched him, he might have picked up traces of Smart Water, too?"

"Well, he might," said Cooper. "But what about the other surveillance measures?"

Udall put down the report. "The what?"

"Kevin Hewitt isn't the only one who's been using digital technology, is he?"

"I —."

"The cameras, Tracy. The CCTV cameras."

An hour later, Udall returned looking pleased with herself. She was carrying a tape which she slid into a VCR.

"You were right, Ben. Nestwatch had a camera set up on a tree that overlooks the approach to the nesting site. Sergeant Jackson retrieved the tape this morning."

Udall pressed the play button and a grainy shot of trees and undergrowth came on to the screen.

"Did it catch Kevin Hewitt approaching the tree?"

"No, we weren't that lucky."

"I bet he'd have known the camera was there, and come in from a different direction."

"Yes, he was canny enough."

Nothing happened for a few minutes. The occasional bird flickered across the screen, a branch swayed jerkily in the breeze.

"Coming up now," said Udall. "Watch the edge of that tree. He comes into shot there, but only briefly. And he's clearly carrying a firearm."

Cooper could see the figure now, unnaturally bulky in a green jacket, brown corduroy trousers, a hat pulled over the ears. Most walkers on the moors dressed in bright colours, so they'd be easy to spot from a distance if they got lost or injured. But some people didn't want to be noticed. It was essential to blend in with the landscape when you went out hunting vermin.

"See him?" asked Udall.

Cooper paused the tape. "Not only do I see him, Tracy. I know him."

"So what do we do?"

"Call out the team."

As soon as he got out of the car, Cooper could feel a fine rain in the air, soft as feathers on his face. Sunlight and showers passed across the hills, clouds moving so quickly across the horizon they were dizzying. For some reason, Udall was wearing her stab-proof vest. A sensible precaution on most occasions, but it looked odd when the most dangerous thing in sight was a gorse bush.

As they drove into the Upper Derwent Valley, the team had been careful not to disturb the peace with their beacons or the wail of their sirens. But now the time for discretion had passed. A Ford estate parked at the visitor centre was boxed in and surrounded. Within minutes, a suspect was sitting in the back of a police Range Rover, twisting his beanie hat in his hands.

"It's harassment. You should be going after the people who kill living animals, not me."

"We just need to clear something up, Mr Ryan," said Cooper. "We're investigating the manslaughter of Mr Kevin Hewitt."

"You're wasting your time. You've got the wrong person."

An officer came across from the Ford, carrying two clear, plastic evidence bags that he showed to Cooper. They contained a BSA Meteor and five tins of Vermin Pell.

"I see you own an air rifle, though, Mr Ryan."

"Well, I never said there was anything wrong with shooting in itself. I'm not one of those animal rights nutters who want to ban all country sports on principle. Is that what you took me for?"

Cooper tried never to give away what he was thinking. It didn't always work, though. You'd need a course at RADA for that, sometimes.

"So you're telling me you try to take a moderate position?"

"I think birds that have legal protection should be protected properly," said Ryan. "Is that a moderate position?"

"It depends."

"And if they're going to be protected properly, that means *someone* has to enforce the law. You lot never do."

"On the contrary, that's exactly what we're going to do now," said Cooper. And he began to issue the caution.

Without even thinking about it, Cooper knew exactly where he'd find Janine Hewitt that afternoon. In the recreation ground on the Devonshire Estate, he could see Jack scuffing about in the grass, as if kicking at a non-existent ball, while Ebony slumped in her pushchair, watching the trees.

Janine had chosen the same bench to sit on, close to the old drinking fountain. Perhaps she preferred it because it was on the north side of the park and caught the best of the sun.

But Janine didn't seem to have noticed the sun. Her eyes were turned downwards, gazing at her shoes. They were the same shoes that she'd bought an eBay — a real bargain, a cheap way to make a bit of a show. She didn't acknowledge Cooper's presence, even when he was standing a few feet away. He waited on the path, trying to assess her mood before he spoke. But it was Janine who finally broke the silence.

"Oh, it's you," she said. "I should have guessed."

She sounded resigned, not disturbed or aggressive. Cooper moved a few steps closer, then stopped and smiled at Jack, who responded with a blank stare.

"You know Kevin won't be coming back, don't you, Janine?"

"Yes, they called me in to identify him."

"I'm sorry."

"Have you caught the person who did it?" she asked, without hope.

"We have a suspect in custody. And... well, we've got some theories on motive."

Janine nodded wearily. "It doesn't matter, does it? I mean — the motive, the 'why'. The result is just the same."

Cooper found he wasn't listening to Janine Hewitt any more. Instead, the voice inside his head was Calvin Ryan's. He was remembering a moment on the windswept edge of Lightside Moor, watching a black shape soar over Alport Castles. And he could hear Ryan saying something. It sounded like *Don't forget the goshawks.*

Janine's four-year-old, Jack, was playing on the grass, running round the old drinking fountain. Though it hadn't been used for years, the fountain was solidly made, and no one had gone to the trouble of digging it out and breaking it up. Cooper could see a hole at the base, where the root of a tree had pushed through the earth and left a dark cavity.

"A bonded pair will hunt co-operatively, two of them together."

As Cooper watched, Jack bent down and peered into the hole, as if expecting to find something interesting. Perhaps he was playing some game of his own imagination. A treasure hunt, who could say? The child looked towards his mother, and for a second an expression of conspiracy passed across his face before he moved on, chuckling at the sight of a blackbird scratching in the dead leaves.

Janine had begun to gather herself together, picking up the toddler's bottle from the seat. The bench she was using was the third one from the gate on the northern side of the park. It was always the same bench that she chose, the one near the old drinking fountain. There was nothing remarkable about the bench itself, that Cooper could see. But it was always the same one.

"Then, when the chicks are hatched, the tercel isn't allowed near the nest. He has to leave the food he catches at a safe distance, where the female bird can fetch it for the chicks."

Cooper pulled his phone out of his pocket. Then he hesitated, surprised by a stab of doubt. Instead of making the call, he left Janine and walked back to his car. For a while, he sat in the driver's seat, trying not to think about anything in particular, until he saw Janine and the children on their way home. Back to their dismal council house, the bedrooms with damp walls and the drug addicts next door. He couldn't imagine what it was like raising two small children in conditions like those.

As soon as they were out of sight, Cooper went back to the park. He followed Jack's footsteps to the drinking fountain, and examined the cavity. Something in there, definitely. It wasn't just a figment of the child's imagination. From the marks on the ground, he guessed there had been dead leaves piled over the hole at one time, but they'd been kicked aside by the blackbirds scratching for insects.

He reached in, grabbed a handful of plastic, and tugged. It was the wrapping of a package, and the plastic rustled as he drew it into the light. To Cooper, the sound seemed very loud in the suddenly silent afternoon.

The package was too big to have fallen into the hole accidentally. Too full of money. When he'd pulled it out, he saw there were hundreds of used notes, held together in bundles by rubber bands and spilling out of a rip in the plastic. It was impossible to say how much money there was. Kevin Hewitt had been gathering it from many sources, perhaps some that would never be uncovered.

Cooper turned, imagining Janine watching him. And not just her, but the children, too — the restless Jack, the lethargic toddler in her pushchair. He could picture them staring at him with those hungry eyes, helpless and desperate.

At his feet lay more money than he could count. Thousands, certainly. Right now, his duty was to call it in, make sure it was secured for evidence before he handled it any further. But what was the point, really? No one would ever come forward to claim the cash. It was a pity, because there were so many uses it could be put to.

Well, Harry Blakelock had been right about one thing. Sometimes you had to choose. There were times when everyone had to take sides.

Cooper straightened up as he looked at the notes. Yes, so many uses. For a start, he bet there was enough money here to put a deposit on a small house, somewhere a lot nicer than the Devonshire Estate. A place well away from the damp and despair, and the junkies.

Enough money, perhaps, to give one family a new start.